GROLIER

Your partner in education

**Distributed by Grolier, Sherman Turnpike
Danbury, Connecticut 06816**

Grolier offers a varied selection of
children's book racks and tote bags.
For details on ordering, please write:
Grolier Direct Marketing
Sherman Turnpike
Danbury, CT 06816
Att: Premium Department

My S Book

by Jane Belk Moncure
illustrated by Linda Hohag

THE CHILD'S WORLD
Mankato, MN 56001

Little  S had a  box.

He said, "I will fill my  box."

 Little S took off his

shoes,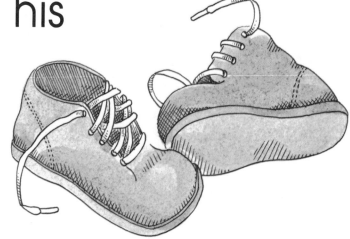

socks,

sweater,

and shirt.

He put them into his box.

Little  put on his swimsuit and his sandals.

Then he went for a walk.

He found  a shovel,
a sand pail,
and a sand castle.

He put them into his box.

Little S went for a swim.

He saw a seal swimming
in the sea.

He saw six seals on the sand.
Did he put them into his box?

He did!

Little s found seashells, lots of seashells.

He found a

starfish too.

"In you go," he said.

Then he saw a
    shark.

He put the shark into
    a sack.

He put the sack
into his box.

Little  saw a sea snake.

He put the sea snake into a sack too.
Do you know why?

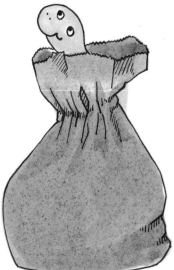

Later Little  S met a sailor.

"Hi," he said.

Guess what the sailor gave him?
A sailor hat.

"You can be a sailor," he said.

They played on
the see-saw.

They slid down the

slide.

They swung in the swings.

Suddenly they heard a loud sound.

"What is in your box?" asked the sailor.

"Things that begin with my sound," said Little S.

23

"I sail on things that begin with your sound," said the sailor.

"I sail on  a ship.

"I sail on a submarine."

Guess what Little  said?
"I want to sail."

Little took

along

his box.

slide

sailor

swing

sandals

seven seals

shoe

shovel

sand
pail

sand castle

What fun they had in the submarine.

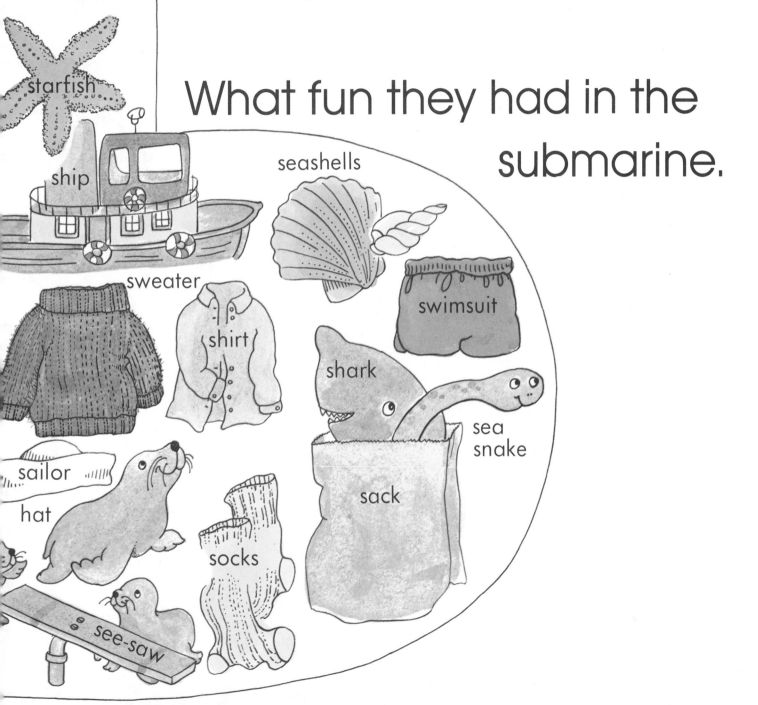

starfish

ship

seashells

sweater

shirt

swimsuit

shark

sea snake

sailor

hat

sack

socks

see-saw

27

More words with Little

sunflower

stick

snail

soap

salad

star

sink

seed

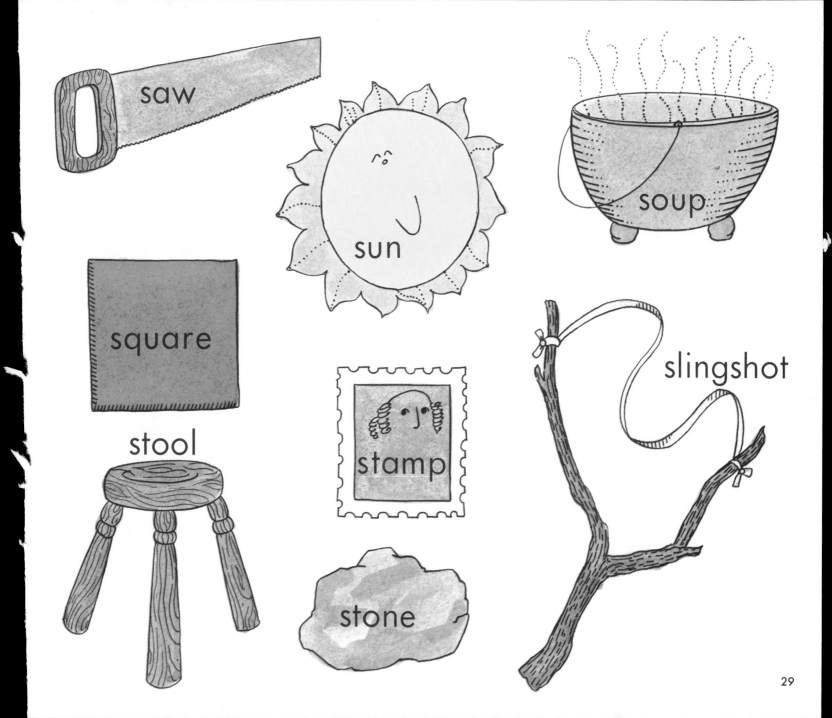

saw

sun

soup

square

stool

stamp

slingshot

stone

29